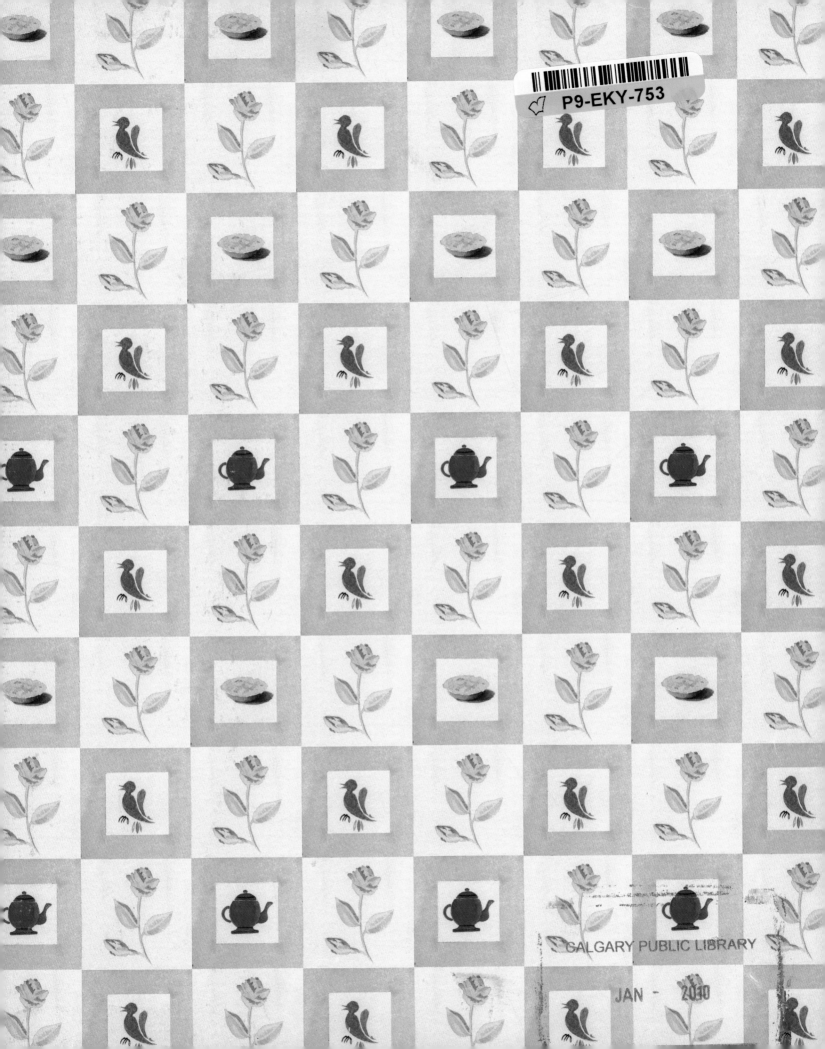

To Violetta Adamidou,
expert home-finder—J. S. W.

To the teachers and students at Lexington Elementary
School in South Carolina and a special thanks
to Lexington County Museum and Libby Ranch
—E. B. L.

MARGARET K. McELDERRY BOOKS

An imprint of Simon & Schuster Children's Publishing Division

1230 Avenue of the Americas, New York, New York 10020

Text copyright © 2009 by Janet S. Wong

Illustrations copyright © 2009 by E. B. Lewis

All rights reserved, including the right of reproduction in whole or in part in any form.

Book design by Debra Sfetsios

The text for this book is set in Celestia Antiqua Std.

The illustrations for this book are rendered in watercolor.

Manufactured in China

10 9 8 7 6 5 4 3 2 1

Library of Congress Cataloging-in-Publication Data

Wong, Janet S.

Homegrown house / by Janet S. Wong ; illustrated by E. B. Lewis.—1st ed.

p. cm.

Summary: A young girl describes her grandmother's comfortable,

long-time home, and wishes she could stay in the same house instead of

moving so often.

ISBN-13: 978-0-689-84718-9 (hardcover)

ISBN-10: 0-689-84718-1 (hardcover)

[1. Home—Fiction. 2. Moving, Household—Fiction. 3. Grandmothers—Fiction.] I. Lewis, Earl B., ill. II. Title.

PZ7.W842115Hom 2009

[E]—dc22

2006038599

homegrown house

by **Janet S. Wong**
illustrated by **E. B. Lewis**

MARGARET K. McELDERRY BOOKS
New York   London   Toronto   Sydney

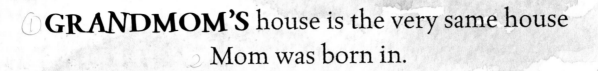 **GRANDMOM'S** house is the very same house
Mom was born in.

Grandmom calls it her **homegrown house**—
says it was nothing much at all
before she came to grow it up
forty years ago
when she left the house where she was born
and moved in with Granddad.

Sixty-five years alive,
and Grandmom's known just two houses,
not counting summers with her cousins.

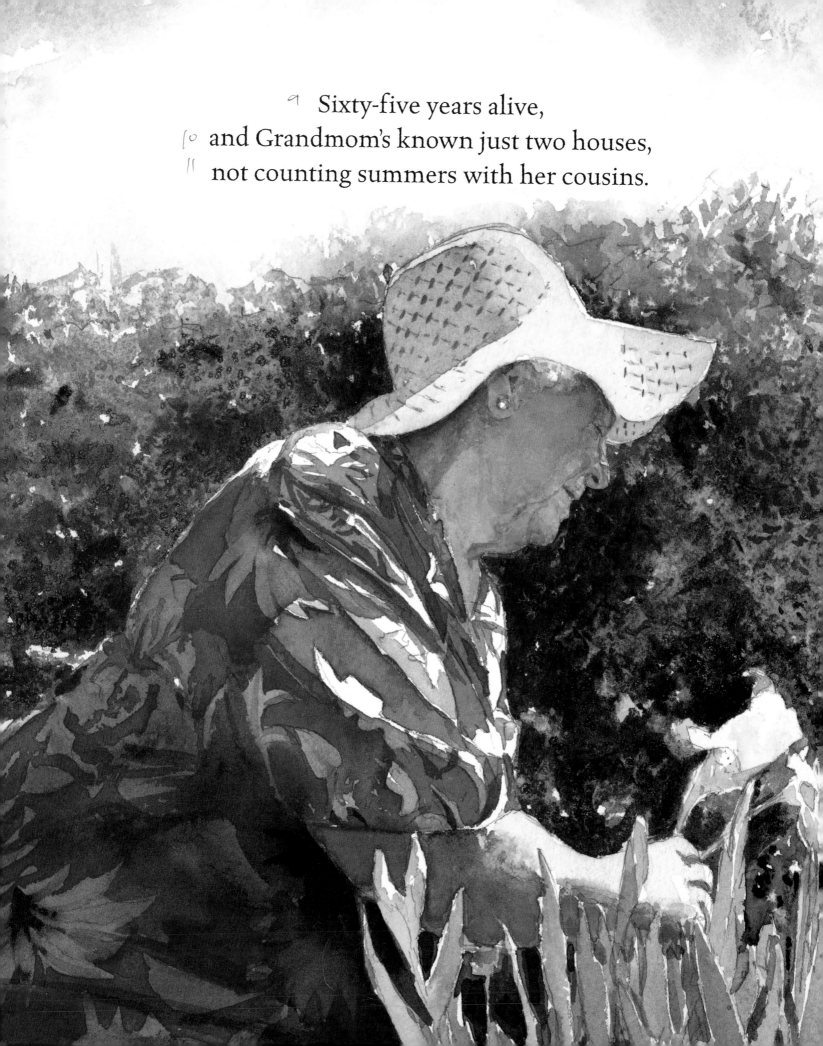

12 I'm eight
13 and already I've lived in three.

14 Grandmom says I'm getting to know
15 a whole lot more of the world
16 than she ever did.

17 That's three times as many friends,
18 lucky you!

19 **Lucky me?**

It took four winters
for the splinters to wear down
on the jungle gym
at my preschool–kindergarten house.

The fort part was finally smooth enough
to sit on in shorts
when Dad decided to take a new job
a whole day's drive away
and we had to move.

29 At that next house,
30 my first grade–second grade house,
31 Mom grew into such a grouch—
32 *What an ugly chain-link fence!*
33 *What nosy neighbors!*

34 Groused so much,
35 Grandmom brought us two dozen fir trees
36 in her neighbor Pearl's pickup truck.
37 It was Christmas in September!

38 Just when the trees finally started to grow up
39 fat and wide
40 to hide the chain link—

41 and me—

42 Mom got a much better job than Dad
43 and we had to move again,
44 but this was all right
45 because we moved to the town next door to Grandmom.

46 Last year
47 I made five best friends here
48 who live a fast run down the hill

49 and last month
50 I put my bookshelf in alphabetical order
51 by title

52 **so we can't move**
53 **now.**

54 But Mom just got a raise
55 and can't hear me talk
56 with her nose stuck
57 in those glossy house magazines.

58 She's so busy dreaming
59 about our brand-new old-fashioned house
60 with its curves and little windows.

61 Or our brand-new modern house
62 with its sharp corners and huge windows.

63 Our brand-new super-huge house
64 with an empty room for the piano
65 (which we don't own yet).

66 Dad's no better,
67 dreaming about the flat grassy yard
68 where I guess I am supposed to play.

69 Dreaming about *something with water*—
70 a pond,
71 a creek in the back,
72 a lake view,
73 the sound of the river.

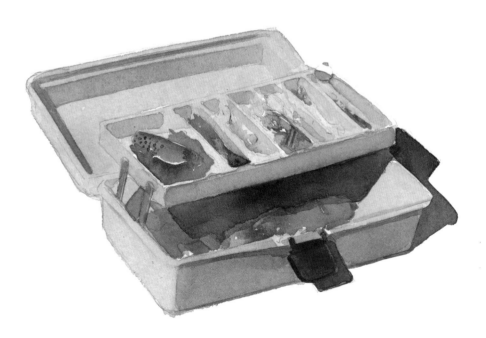

74 Grandmom says,
75 *The sound of the river makes me have to pee—*
76 *and who's going to mow all that grass*
77 *is what I want to know!*

78 Grandmom says it takes time
79 to settle into a house,
80 to learn to love it right,
81 to make it feel homegrown.
82 Thirty years should do it.

83 When I tell Mom and Dad

84 I don't want to move again,

85 Mom twists her mouth up and says,

86 *Don't you want a better house?*

87 Dad says,

88 *Wouldn't it be great:*

89 *first thing in the morning*

90 *you'd wake up and see*

91 *morning dewdrops on the lawn and*

92 *mist on the lake.*

93 More than anything else

94 what I love to see

95 first thing in the morning is

96 a plate of hash browns

97 with two blueberry waffles,

98 lots of butter and syrup.

99 And a chocolate shake!

Mmmmmmmmmm—
I love breakfast at Grandmom's!

I like having Grandmom along
on House Hunt Sundays.

Can't have that house!
Twenty years ago
I watched that child grow up
and the way she used to pick her nose and put it
all over the everywhere—

This weekend
we've seen a dozen houses,
one after another,
and none the way they read in the paper.

This house here should say,
Strange house on noisy street,
awful bathroom tile!

116 I hate walking through people's houses
117 when they're not there—

118 teddy bears peeking at me
119 from behind the pillows,
120 chocolate-chip cookies calling my name
121 from tight glass jars.

122 I especially hate the houses
123 where all they bake in the oven
124 is a pot full of vanilla *soup!*

125 The very best house I've ever been in
126 is Grandmom's house.

127 A dozen different colors on the walls,
128 the kitchen a warm butter yellow
129 to make you hungry.

130 The bedrooms mossy green
131 so you can pretend you're hibernating.

132 Closets spilling—
133 **surprises!**

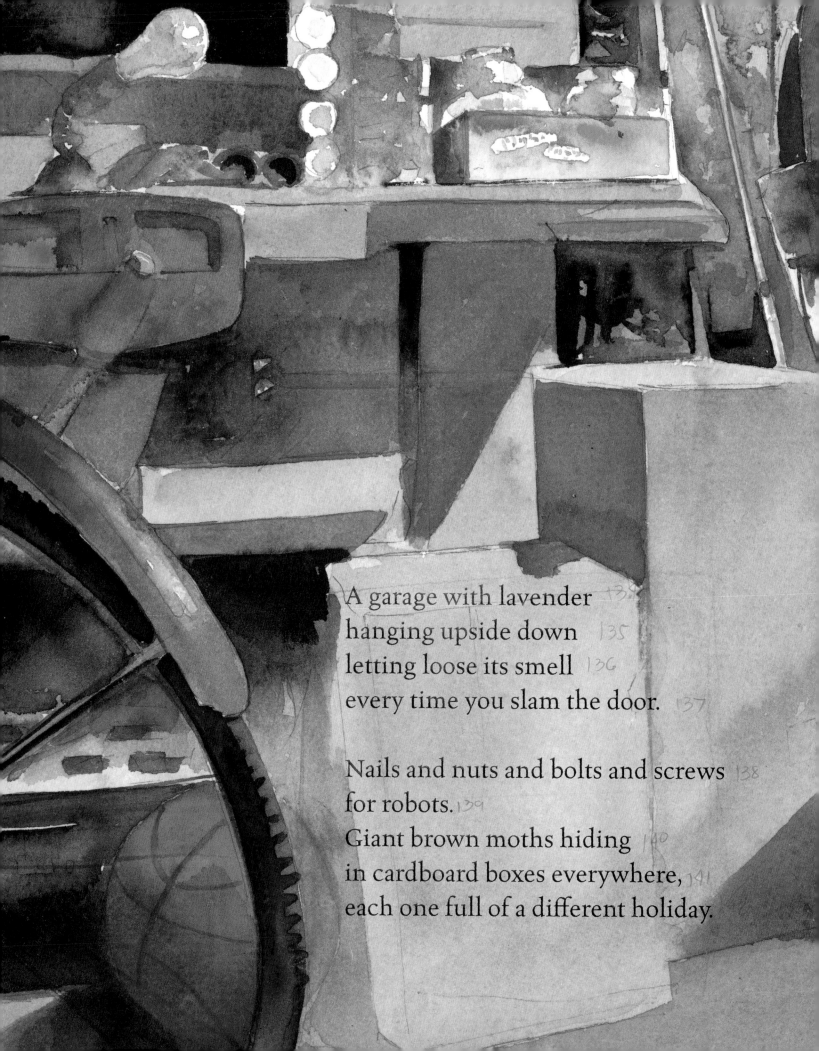

A garage with lavender
hanging upside down
letting loose its smell
every time you slam the door.

Nails and nuts and bolts and screws
for robots.
Giant brown moths hiding
in cardboard boxes everywhere,
each one full of a different holiday.

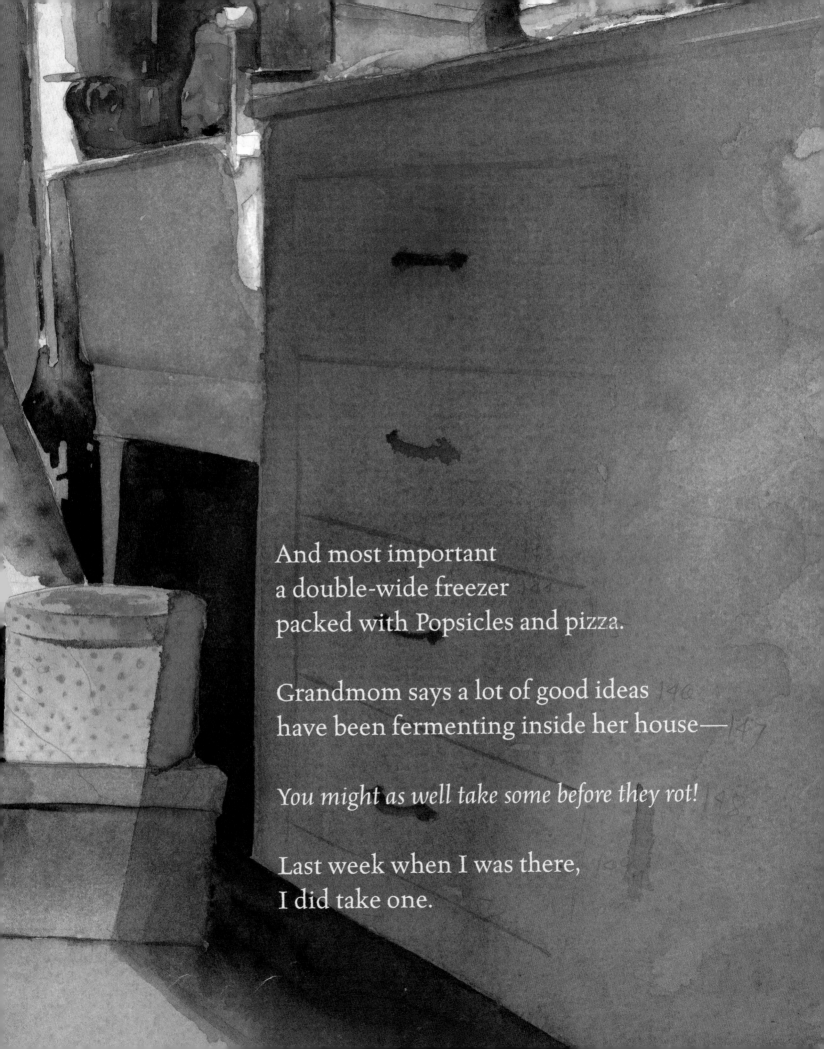

And most important
a double-wide freezer
packed with Popsicles and pizza.

Grandmom says a lot of good ideas
have been fermenting inside her house—

You might as well take some before they rot!

Last week when I was there,
I did take one.

It's not a flat grassy yard
but I can see it in my mind.

A whole meadow's worth of wildflowers
on the steep slope behind our house.
Bunches of dried lavender hanging upside down
from the ceiling of my bedroom,
which will be painted five different colors
including rainbow tie-dye.

Oh yes,
Grandmom's house gives you room
to think.

162 And today
163 I came up with a second idea.

164 Back behind the shed
165 where Mom thinks the mice hide,

166 I am going to make a pond
167 two feet deep and ten feet wide,
168 deeper if my friends help dig
169 (and I hope they will)—

170 I'll put watercress and goldfish in it,
171 the spitting angel Grandmom bought
172 for five dollars at her church sale,
173 a handful of tadpoles too.

And after we empty our storage garage,
unpack all our cardboard boxes,
let our giant moths loose,

and fill the freezer with Popsicles and pizza,

there will be nothing more to do—

Nothing except

to settle into this house,
to learn to love it right,
to make it feel,

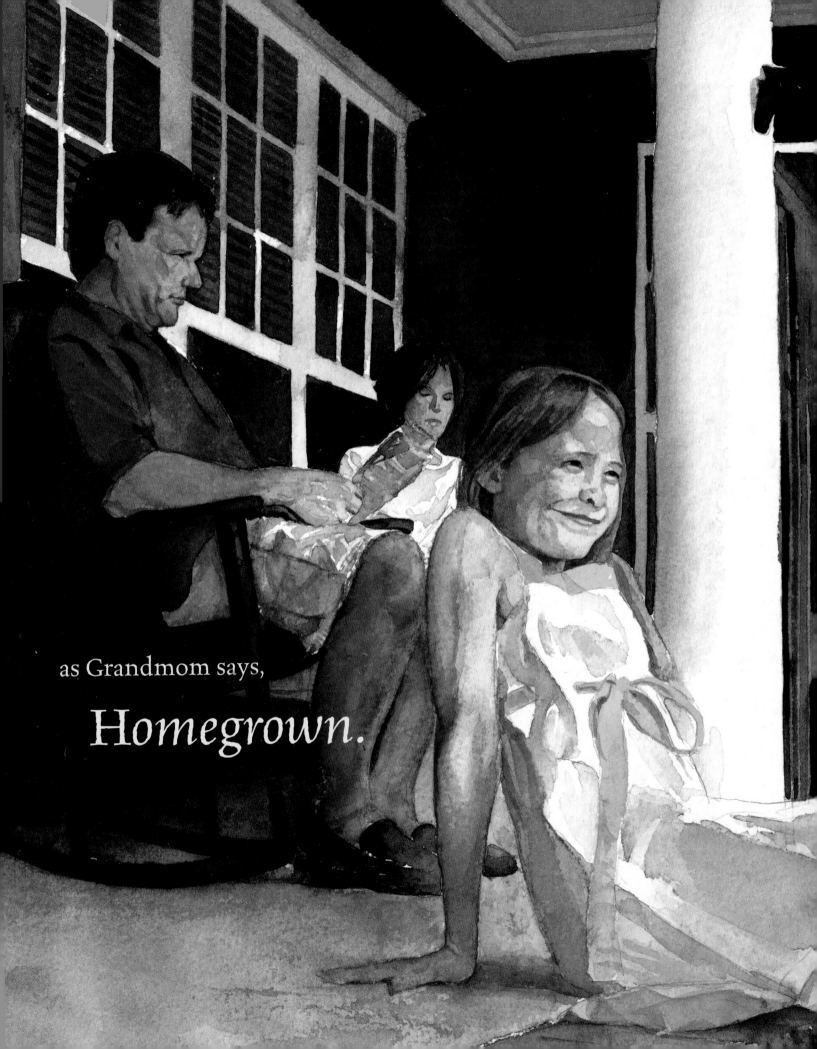

as Grandmom says,

Homegrown.